SOUTH PACIFIC

as told by

James A. Michener

ILLUSTRATED BY

Michael Hague

BASED ON
RODGERS AND HAMMERSTEIN'S
South Pacific

GULLIVER BOOKS
HARCOURT BRACE JOVANOVICH, PUBLISHERS
San Diego   New York   London

Library of Congress Cataloging-in-Publication Data
Michener, James A. (James Albert), 1907–
South Pacific/as told by James A. Michener;
illustrated by Michael Hague. — 1st ed.
p.   cm.
"Gulliver books."
"Based on Rodgers and Hammerstein's South Pacific."
Summary: A retelling of the story of the musical "South Pacific,"
concerning the lives of officers, nurses, a French expatriate,
and natives on the islands of the South Pacific during World War II.
Includes discussion of the original Broadway production and its cast.
ISBN 0-15-200618-4
ISBN 0-15-200615-X (ltd. ed.)
[1. World War, 1939–1945 — Campaigns — Pacific Area — Fiction.
2. South Pacific Ocean — Fiction. 3. Musicals — Stories, plots, etc.]
I. Hague, Michael, ill.   II. Rodgers, Richard, 1902–1979 — South Pacific.
III. Title.
PZ7.M581917So   1992
[Fic] — dc20   91-28934

First edition
A B C D E

The illustrations in this book were done in pen-and-ink
and watercolor on Crescent cold-press watercolor board.
The display type was set in Florentine and the text type
in Linotype Walbaum by Thompson Type, San Diego, California.
Color separations were made by Bright Arts, Ltd., Singapore.
Printed and bound by Tien Wah Press, Singapore
Production supervision by Warren Wallerstein and Ginger Boyer
Designed by Michael Farmer

To the memory of two notable artists,
Richard Rodgers and Oscar Hammerstein
— J. A. M.

To Riley
— M. H.

THE WORLD was at war. In every corner of the earth great battles were being fought. One of the most important struggles took place among the beautiful islands of the South Pacific Ocean. Here, two powerful nations, Japan and the United States, faced each other in deadly combat.

Our story takes place on one of these islands. It was an exotic tropical paradise populated by French planters and the native Tonkinese. On this little island, in the midst of World War II, a smaller war was taking place. It was a strange war, one that placed the importance of true love against the racial prejudice taught back home.

STATIONED on this beautiful island, surrounded by quiet beaches and tall palm trees, was a group of sailors, aviators, and Navy nurses, waiting and preparing for battle. One day a plane brought a newcomer to their camp. He was Lieutenant Joe Cable, a young, handsome Marine officer from Philadelphia who was both courageous and eager to help his country win the war. He had been assigned to travel to a nearby island called Marie Louise and spy on Japanese activities there. With the information Cable sent back, the Americans would be ready for the next attack.

Cable already knew who he wanted to help him with this secret mission. The man was Emile de Becque, a French plantation owner who had once lived on Marie Louise and who knew the islands well. De Becque's knowledge could be invaluable to the success of the mission. But Cable had heard rumors that de Becque had killed a man and, since the mission was dangerous and the two men could lose their lives, Cable needed to know if de Becque was trustworthy. His first job was to find out all he could about Emile de Becque.

One of the people Cable met in his first days at the camp was Ensign Nellie Forbush, a pretty Navy nurse with short brown hair and sparkling eyes from Little Rock, Arkansas. She was as different from Joe Cable as one could get. Joe was a college man from a prestigious family in a large Northern city. Nellie did not have wealthy parents, and she had grown up in a small city in the South. Although she had not attended college, she had a wonderful common sense and seemed to understand people very well. While Joe Cable often kept to himself, Nellie was always in the middle of things, having fun. Her bubbly personality had made her very popular. Most important to Cable, she was very much in love with Emile de Becque. Perhaps she could tell Cable whether de Becque could be trusted.

Nellie had first met Emile de Becque at a Navy dance where she was, as always, the most popular of all the girls. The young officers loved her cheerfulness, her ability to make friends with everyone, and her willingness to share the heat and mosquitoes without complaint. They all wanted to dance with her.

During one dance she happened to look across the crowded room and see a man staring at her. He could not be an American; he was not in uniform. When she asked who he was, one of her fellow nurses whispered, "He's a Frenchman and owns the biggest plantation on the island. His name's Emile de Becque."

At the same time the Frenchman, much older than the young officers, asked one of them, "Who is that marvelous nurse out there on the floor?" The American replied, "We call her Nurse Nellie, our Cockeyed Optimist. She's from Little Rock, Arkansas."

When the dance ended, Nellie looked again at Emile de Becque. He was still watching her, as if enchanted. When the music started again,

he turned to her. Not waiting for him to ask for the next dance, she moved toward him. They danced together proudly and gracefully, as if in a dream. In the days that followed, they saw each other constantly. Soon the whole island knew they were in love.

After that night, Nellie often visited Emile's home atop a hill covered with flowers. There she met Jerome and Ngana, two delightful children who she thought belonged to the Tonkinese people who worked on the plantation. Jerome and Ngana were adorable and seemed to have a special relationship with Emile. This made Nellie love Emile even more. He was different from anyone she'd ever known. Far away from her home in Little Rock, Nellie began to feel she could be happy for the rest of her life with Emile on his majestic plantation.

But when she talked about him with the other nurses, they warned her, "Nellie! You don't know much about this Frenchman. Be careful. Don't fall in love with him before you find out who he is."

So one day when Emile invited her to picnic beside the sea, she asked him bluntly, "Why are you living alone on this island? Why did you leave France?" He answered honestly, "I killed a man and had to flee." That was all he said. Nellie was not alarmed and asked no more questions. She was sure that if Emile had killed a man he had done so for a very good reason.

Nellie thought little more about this conversation until one day, soon after the picnic, she was called to a meeting with Joe Cable and two other officers.

"Nellie, we need you to help us," one of the officers said. "We have heard that your friend Emile de Becque killed a man. We need you to find out why." Nellie was troubled. Spy on Emile? How could she spy on

the man she loved? She wished she understood why they wanted to know, but she couldn't ask. She had been given orders and she had to follow them.

By now, Joe Cable had met other people on the island. Among them were Luther Billis, one of the sailors, and Bloody Mary, a roly-poly Tonkinese woman. Luther and Bloody Mary had much in common. They were both opportunists, using the war and the presence of the nurses and sailors on the island to make money for themselves. Luther did laundry for pay and made souvenirs for Bloody Mary to sell to the other sailors. In addition Bloody Mary sold shrunken heads, boar's teeth bracelets, and grass skirts brought from a nearby island.

Luther was a loud and raucous man with a big ship tattooed on his stomach. By breathing in and out he could make the ship look as if it were sailing. All the sailors loved to watch his antics, and Luther's business was good.

One day Luther said to Cable, "See that island in the mists over there? It's magical."

"What do you mean?" Cable asked.

Luther explained, "It's called Bali Ha'i, and it's a very exciting and mysterious place. Today they're having a boar's tooth festival. Would you like to go with me?"

"No. Anyway, I couldn't go unless I had a boat," Cable answered.

Luther quickly responded, "I can get you one."

Cable was feeling frustrated with the interminable waiting to go to Marie Louise. At last he agreed to go to Bali Ha'i. So Luther stole a boat—he could steal almost anything—and he took Cable to see the

magical island. Bali Ha'i was certainly beautiful. It rose out of the ocean like a small mountain, lush with palm trees and surrounded by an eerie mist that changed color as the sun moved over it.

Bloody Mary was waiting for Luther and Cable at the dock. She liked Cable and she had her own secret plan. He's the perfect man to marry my daughter Liat, she thought. But to Cable she simply said, "Lieutenant Cable, you're one handsome man!" All day Mary watched Cable closely, and when he finally tired of the festival, she led him to a grass shack where her beautiful golden-skinned daughter Liat was waiting.

"Is she not lovely?" Bloody Mary asked slyly. Cable took one look at

Liat and immediately fell in love with the exquisite girl. She had long shining dark hair, skin as smooth as silk, and soft, shy eyes. When it was time to leave, Luther had to call Cable many times before he would tear himself away from Liat.

In the days that followed, Luther Billis took Cable back to Bali Ha'i many times to visit with Liat. During those visits their love grew stronger. Bloody Mary was happy as she watched the young people, and she told friends, "Lieutenant Cable's gonna marry my daughter."

One afternoon, while Cable was with Liat, Nellie found out from Emile what she needed to know. He finally told her the whole story of how he came to kill a man. The man had attacked Emile in the public square of their town. Emile fought back and the man fell to the ground. His head struck a stone and he died immediately. Not knowing what else to do, Emile fled, never to return to France. When Emile finished this story, Nellie was relieved. She knew Emile was truly as good and kind as she had thought; he had only been defending himself. More than ever she wanted to marry him.

When Nellie told the officers and Cable what she knew, they were also relieved, but for a very different reason. De Becque *was* the perfect man to accompany Cable on the mission to Marie Louise. He knew the island well. And now they were convinced he was as brave and strong as they needed him to be. After Nellie left the meeting, messengers were sent to fetch de Becque.

When he arrived, the officers told de Becque, "Our nation has been losing this war. Now we have a chance to win a great victory that might help us to turn the tide of the war. Would you be willing to take a great risk to help us win that victory?"

"What risk?" de Becque asked suspiciously.

"Here's the plan. You will get in a plane with Cable here. Take a radio with you. Parachute into Marie Louise Island and send us news of what the enemy is about to do. With that news, we can be prepared to stop their ships."

Cable stepped forward and looked at de Becque. "You told me the other day you used to have a plantation on Marie Louise. You're the only one who can help."

Everyone stared at Emile de Becque, waiting for him to agree to go. But instead he surprised them all. He was thinking not of Marie Louise Island, but of Nurse Nellie Forbush, and he said solemnly, "When a man lives alone on an island he dreams that someday a beautiful woman will come along to make him happy. Such a woman has come to my island. She brings a strong promise of happiness, which I cannot risk losing."

"You refuse to go?" the officers asked.

"Yes. My happiness is here. Get someone else to fight your war." De Becque marched out of the meeting.

When he was gone, the senior officer said, "I know he's not a coward. But can he be sure that Nurse Forbush will want to marry him when she finds out that the two children she thinks are Tonkinese are actually his own? She's from Arkansas, you know, and she will not be happy as the stepmother of two native children."

That night Emile invited Nellie to his plantation for a grand dinner party. He wanted her to meet his friends, the French men and women who lived on the island. When Nellie arrived, they all welcomed her with embraces and the wish that she find happiness in her forthcom-

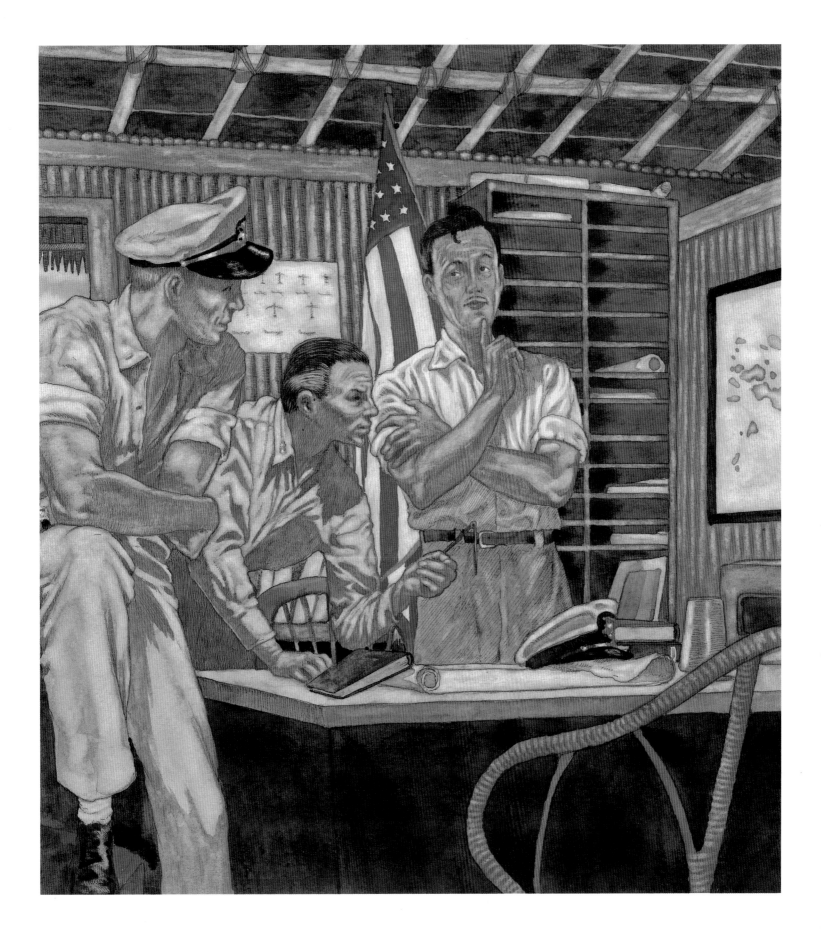

ing marriage with their friend Emile. The dinner party was a gala affair, with dancing, fine food from the plantation, and wines from France. Emile was never more handsome and Nellie was charming in her white evening dress.

As she danced, Nellie thought, When peace comes, living on this island with Emile would be much more exciting than going back to Little Rock. Whirling about as if she had wings, she whispered to him, "I love you. I want to live here with you."

When the guests left and the lovers were alone, Emile told Nellie, "I have a surprise for you." Suddenly Jerome and Ngana appeared on the terrace to wish her good night.

"You are so beautiful," Nellie exclaimed as she hugged and kissed them.

Then they ran to Emile and hugged him, too. "Good night, Papa," they giggled. When they were gone, Nellie turned to Emile. "Emile, why do they call you Papa? Whose children are they?" she asked.

"Nellie, they are my children," Emile answered. "Their mother is dead."

Nellie was astounded. She had thought they were the children of the Tonkinese working on the plantation. But now she was being told that Emile had had a "native" wife. She ran to the edge of the terrace with tears in her eyes. Emile followed her. "Nellie, their mother is dead. She was a Polynesian woman and was very beautiful."

"How could you?" Nellie asked.

"I loved her very much," Emile answered.

Quickly Nellie grabbed her navy blue cape, threw it about her shoulders, and ran toward her jeep.

"Nellie! Come back!" Emile shouted.

"I—I can't," Nellie stammered and drove quickly away so Emile would not see her sobbing. Her marriage was impossible. She had been brought up to believe that white men had to marry white women. She couldn't be a mother to half-Polynesian children. And she could not marry a man who had had a Polynesian wife.

While Nellie was alone in her tent, weeping over her loss of Emile, Joe Cable was suffering his own heartache. He had fallen very much in love with Liat, but that afternoon Bloody Mary had told him some startling news. "Liat will marry a plantation owner if you don't agree to marry her yourself."

Joe hesitated. "Mary, I can't." He knew that he could never take Liat back to Philadelphia. The picture of Bloody Mary meeting his aunts and uncles dismayed him. Liat looked stricken. Before she could say a word, Mary grabbed her daughter's hand and dragged her away.

Joe returned from Bali Ha'i that night with a heavy heart. When he reached his tent he could think of no one else. Liat was more graceful than a swan, more beautiful than a dream. He had never known a love as powerful as this, but he knew he could not marry her.

The next morning Emile de Becque the French planter agreed to join Joe Cable the fighting Marine on the most dangerous journey of their lives. They felt they had nothing more to lose and immediately

began making plans for the mission. As they worked, Emile asked Joe, "How can you and Nellie let your prejudices get in the way of your love?"

"We were taught to be this way," was all Joe could answer.

As planned, they would fly in a small plane to Marie Louise Island, jump out of the plane with parachutes, hide in the jungle, and send radio messages back to headquarters. There was little doubt that the Japanese would quickly learn they were on the island and send troops and planes to try to kill them. But if de Becque and Cable could hide for seven or eight days, they could gather enough valuable information to help win the war. They were courageous to try.

As the plane flew over Marie Louise, Cable and de Becque surveyed their destination. How were they to land without being seen? Suddenly they were distracted by a commotion in the luggage compartment. To their surprise, out stumbled Luther Billis.

Cable was furious. "How dare you sneak aboard this plane. This is a secret mission!"

"I wanted to help, sir," Luther responded sheepishly.

"Well, you shouldn't be here!" Cable shouted, moving toward Luther.

Stepping back, Luther tripped and suddenly fell through the open door of the plane. Although his parachute carried him safely to the sea, the Japanese had spotted him. Without planning to, Luther had created the perfect diversion.

While another plane flew to rescue Luther, the plane carrying Cable and de Becque sneaked around to the other side of the island and delivered the two men safely into the heart of the jungle. There they built a

hut in the trees, set up their radio, and started sending valuable news back to headquarters. Their job was to hide and to stay alive.

Life in the jungle on Marie Louise was exciting and dangerous. Cable and de Becque reported the movements of the Japanese ships from their hiding place. They moved around from place to place so the Japanese could not find them. But all day planes flew overhead, searching, and enemy troops drew closer. In each new hiding place Joe and Emile talked of Liat and Nellie. One day as they spoke, an ominous noise hummed overhead. "Enemy planes!" Emile shouted. Powerful bombs exploded around the tree hut.

Back on the big island the Americans worked night and day. Orders

had come: "Move out and capture Marie Louise Island from the enemy." Trucks carried guns to cargo ships. Cooks packed their kitchens for the move north. Airplanes loaded fighting men for the first big battle. And soldiers crowded into fifty huge troop ships. Only the hospital in which Nellie worked would stay on the big island. America was finally going to win the war.

The men about to enter battle had been helped enormously by the radio broadcasts from Joe Cable. They knew what the enemy was doing and what its weak spots were. Officers listening to Joe's reports said, "Those two men are the heroes of this battle."

But one day Joe did not come to the microphone as usual. Instead the listeners heard de Becque say sadly, "Yesterday my friend Joe Cable was killed by enemy bombs. I have never known a braver man."

When Nurse Nellie heard the news, she grieved that Joe was dead. Although the mission had been secret, she now knew that Emile had gone off to Marie Louise with Joe. For days she had been able to think of nothing else, and for the first time she was really afraid. What if Emile died, too? Walking alone, she prayed, "Dear God, bring him back. I want to marry him and adopt his children as my own." As she turned to go back she met Bloody Mary and Liat coming to meet her. "What's the news about Lieutenant Cable?" Mary asked. Nellie looked sadly at Liat. "He was killed in battle." The three women held one another and wept.

Nellie spent the next days worrying and waiting. The American troops continued to leave. Nellie was told she could go back to the States, but she begged to be allowed to stay. She could not leave Emile's children alone without their father.

"You will have to learn to mind me," she told Ngana and Jerome. "I'm going to be on this island for a long, long time."

One afternoon, as they were eating lunch on Emile's terrace, the children saw a jeep driving toward the plantation. The jeep stopped and out climbed one of the pilots. Behind him sat Emile.

"Papa! Papa!" The children ran to the jeep and threw their arms around Emile. Over their heads Emile stared at Nellie questioningly. Nellie stared back and slowly smiled. "Welcome to our home, Emile."

STORYTELLER'S NOTE

The miracle of South Pacific, *one of the most popular musical plays ever to reach Broadway, is that two gifted artists, Richard Rodgers the musician and Oscar Hammerstein the poet, borrowed two short stories from a book I wrote about World War II in the Pacific and converted them into a full-length play. Not only did they create a well-crafted drama with a beguiling heroine, a charismatic hero, and a rowdy bunch of sailors, they also produced a magical set of songs, some half-dozen of which became all-time favorites.*

I had written the book under difficult conditions. Stationed as a Navy officer on a remote tropical island with the Japanese enemy not far away, I went to an empty Quonset hut at eleven each night after work, and with a lantern for light and a mosquito bomb to ward off insects, I sat at an old typewriter and two-fingered my way through images of the war about me. I recalled our victories in the air, Japanese victories at sea, the bravery of men, their loneliness, their reactions to the jungle about them. In time, these memories became stories and, later, the stories became a world-famous musical . . . and I was astonished.

When South Pacific *opened in New York on Thursday night, 7 April 1949, at the Majestic Theater, it seemed that spring itself had flooded the stage with flowers, melodies, and the troubled behavior of real-life Americans caught overseas in a devastating global war. It was a mix of realism and fantasy that could rarely be equaled. New York exploded the next morning with news that a smash musical had hit town, and the popular newsman Walter Winchell baptized it with a lucky nickname that stuck:* South Terrific.

The musical earned its fame because of two unusual features. First, it offered sharp dramatic and musical comment on one of America's critical problems, race relations. Twice the plot touched this theme. Nellie Forbush, the country girl from Arkansas, falls in love with Emile de Becque, the glamorous French planter, but ends their relationship when she finds that he has fathered two children by a native wife, now dead. She is incapable of picturing herself married to a man who'd been married earlier to a Polynesian wife.

As if that were not provocative enough, the authors also told the story of young Marine Lieutenant Joe Cable, from a proper family in Philadelphia, who falls in love with the splendid Tonkinese daughter of the riotous Bloody Mary. He wants to marry her, but the prospect of taking such a girl back to Philadelphia terrifies him.

Strangely, and this is one of the unexpected virtues of South Pacific, *it is the southerner, Nellie, who solves the problem by marrying her French planter and adopting as her own his two half-Polynesian children. The northerner, Joe Cable, is unequal to the task of reversing his prejudices. He abandons his island girl, but prior to his death he may have had a change of heart, too late.*

The second unusual feature of the play's success concerned its male lead. To play their romantic hero, Emile de Becque, the authors had chosen a man in his fifties, but one as attractive as any twenty-year-old star. Ezio Pinza, born in Italy, was already a famous operatic basso, beloved in the opera houses La Scala in Milan and the Metropolitan in New York. Larger than life, he was a handsome, athletic man who in his youth had been a bicycle champion. In his maturity, he was recognized as one of the world's premier opera stars. He still had a voice that could make the rafters rumble and listeners' hearts beat faster. He made older men throughout the world say to themselves: I still have a chance. To have cast Pinza in this crucial role was daring; to watch him succeed so overwhelmingly was delightful.

Of course, the abiding star of South Pacific *was the saucy heroine, Nurse Nellie Forbush, played by that remarkable and durable star of the American musical theater, Mary Martin from Weathersford, Texas. Like Pinza, she was ideal for the role. She filled the stage with her antics, dancing on overturned boats, gallivanting in the Thanksgiving amateur theatricals, and above all giving herself that boisterous shampoo right on stage. She was adorable as the corn-fed gal from Little Rock, Arkansas, who won the hearts of the nation.*

There were other dazzling performers: Myron McCormick, male master of the danse du ventre *(belly dance) and Juanita Hall, who sang Bloody Mary with all the glory of a great African-American spiritual. But the brooding spirit of the musical was the incandescent director, Josh Logan, who, with theatrical flair, made the play so much his own that he went on to direct the motion picture.*

Through the inspired efforts of many talented artists, a musical play of marvelous beauty and emotional power was put together. As you read these words and study the artwork, try also to listen to the music. It sings of love and valor.